Barbie through the Decades

Barbie
in the 1980s

DiscoverRoo
An Imprint of Pop!
popbooksonline.com

by Elizabeth Andrews

WELCOME TO DiscoverRoo!

This book is filled with videos, puzzles, games, and more! Scan the QR codes* while you read, or visit the website below to make this book pop.

popbooksonline.com/eighties

abdobooks.com

Published by Pop!, a division of ABDO, PO Box 398166, Minneapolis, Minnesota 55439. Copyright © 2025 by Abdo Consulting Group, Inc. International copyrights reserved in all countries. No part of this book may be reproduced in any form without written permission from the publisher. DiscoverRoo™ is a trademark and logo of Pop!.

Printed in the United States of America, North Mankato, Minnesota.
052024
082024

THIS BOOK CONTAINS RECYCLED MATERIALS

Cover Photo: Shutterstock Images
Interior Photos: Getty Images, Shutterstock Images, Design Bay Productions, MATTEL/SIPA/Newscom, DOOLEY JOHN/SIPA/Newscom
Editor: Grace Hansen
Series Designer: Victoria Bates

Library of Congress Control Number: 2023947575

Publisher's Cataloging-in-Publication Data
Names: Andrews, Elizabeth, author.
Title: Barbie in the 1980s / by Elizabeth Andrews
Description: Minneapolis, Minnesota : Pop!, 2025 | Series: Barbie through the decades | Includes online resources and index
Identifiers: ISBN 9781098246273 (lib. bdg.) | ISBN 9781098246839 (ebook)
Subjects: LCSH: Barbie dolls--Juvenile literature. | Toys--History--Juvenile literature. | Nineteen eighties--Juvenile literature. | Toys--Social aspects--Juvenile literature. | Popular Culture--Juvenile literature.
Classification: DDC 688.722--dc23

*Scanning QR codes requires a web-enabled smart device with a QR code reader app and a camera.

TABLE OF Contents

CHAPTER 1
Barbie's Beginnings............ 4

CHAPTER 2
Living in the Real World......... 10

CHAPTER 3
Eighties Barbie Fashion......... 16

CHAPTER 4
Iconic Barbies.................. 22

Making Connections............ 30
Glossary 31
Index......................... 32
Online Resources 32

CHAPTER 1
Barbie's Beginnings

Humans have made dolls for thousands of years. At first, dolls were made of clay, straw, or other natural materials. As the world changed, so did dolls. The toys got more detailed and exciting. In 1959, the fashion doll, Barbie, hit store shelves. The doll game was never the same.

WATCH A VIDEO HERE!

Barbie's original striped swimsuit was inspired by fashions worn in the 1950s.

Ruth Handler was the creator of Barbie. Ruth and her husband owned the toy company Mattel Creations. Ruth noticed that children's dolls were mostly baby dolls. She believed growing girls didn't want to play with babies. They wanted dolls that encouraged them to dream of their futures.

Ruth Handler was born in Denver, Colorado, in 1916.

Mattel released the first Barbie in 1959. She wore a black-and-white swimsuit, black high heels, white sunglasses, and gold earrings. Barbie was a teenage fashion model from Willows, Wisconsin. She cost $3. Her extra outfits ranged between $1 and $5.

The Handler family

DID YOU KNOW? Barbie's full name is Barbara Millicent Roberts. She was named after Ruth's daughter Barbara.

The first Barbie commercial played during an episode of The Mickey Mouse Club.

Barbie was a hit! In the first year, Mattel sold 350,000 dolls. Soon customers were asking for more. Mattel went on to create friends, dreamhouses, cars, and more than 250 careers for Barbie. Ruth was right. Children did like grown-up dolls. Their imaginations grew with Barbie!

The first Barbie appeared passive and gentle. She fit into the late 1950s female tradition of **homemaking** and beauty **trends**. Some of the first Barbies included Barbie Learns to Cook and Suburban Shopper Barbie. However, Ruth wouldn't keep Barbie in the home for long.

Suburban Shopper Barbie, 1959

CHAPTER 2
Living in the Real World

The 1980s was a decade that brought about big change! It was a time of **materialism** and glamour. **Baby boomers** filled the workforce. They were college educated and making a lot of money. Boomers were known for having expensive taste.

LEARN MORE HERE!

DID YOU KNOW?

The term "yuppie" was used for a young person working in a city. It was short for "young urban professional."

Some women worked in the stock market. It was a fast-paced, high-stress career.

New and exciting products popped up throughout the '80s. Personal computers were becoming common. **Pagers**, portable audio players, boomboxes, and televisions were in most households.

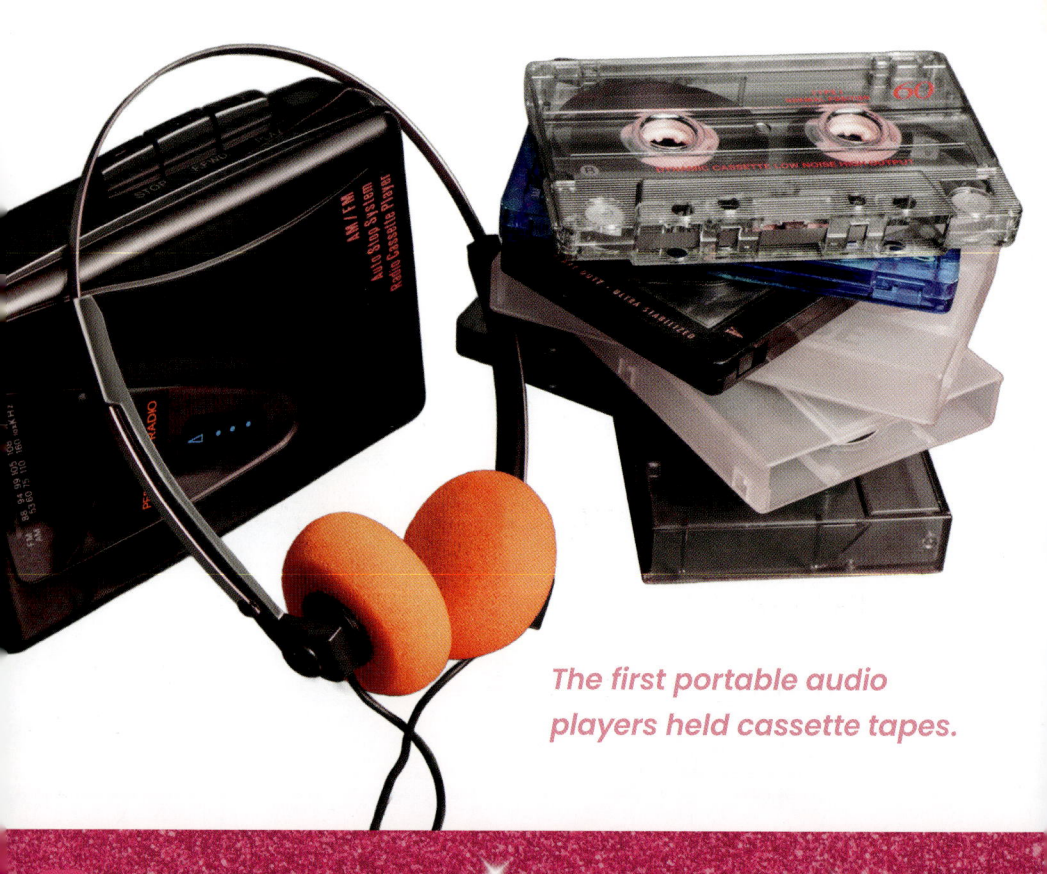

The first portable audio players held cassette tapes.

Bob Pittman helped launch MTV on August 1, 1981.

Television was the main entertainment in the '80s. Cable television brought new ways to discover world news, watch sports, and even listen to music. MTV debuted in 1981. It showed music videos. Young people could watch their favorite music stars from their living rooms.

Ronald Reagan was the 40th President of the United States. He served from 1981 to 1989.

The United States military wasn't involved in any major conflicts in the 1980s. But it did send troops around the world throughout the decade. The military attempted to rescue US citizens taken **hostage** in Iran. The United States also invaded Panama in 1989.

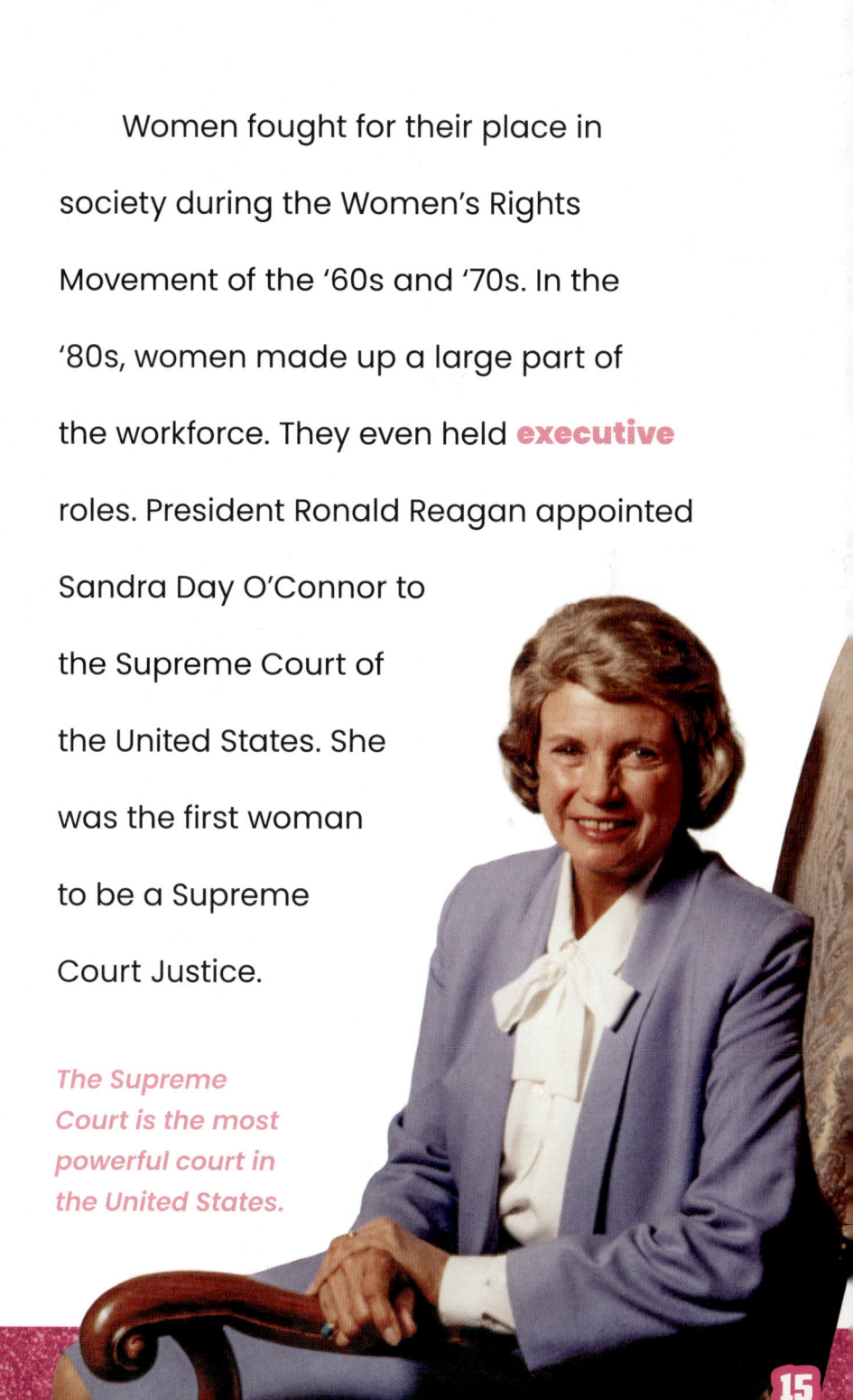

Women fought for their place in society during the Women's Rights Movement of the '60s and '70s. In the '80s, women made up a large part of the workforce. They even held **executive** roles. President Ronald Reagan appointed Sandra Day O'Connor to the Supreme Court of the United States. She was the first woman to be a Supreme Court Justice.

The Supreme Court is the most powerful court in the United States.

CHAPTER 3

Eighties Barbie Fashion

In the 1980s, bigger was often better! This was especially true when it came to accessories, such as belts and bows. Shirt sleeves were large and puffy with padded shoulders. Makeup was colorful. With the arrival of MTV, young people wanted to look like their favorite stars.

EXPLORE LINKS HERE!

Crystal Barbie, 1983, came in a box that said, "She shines with glamour!"

Crystal, Peaches 'n Cream, and Golden Dream Barbies best represented the glamour of the dolls released in the 1980s. They each wore beautiful outfits and had big hairstyles. These exciting looks were seen on real celebrities at the time.

Peaches 'n Cream Barbie, 1985

Sweet Roses Barbie on lunchbox, 1989

Famous stars walked the runway wearing look-alikes of Oscar de la Renta's Barbie fashions.

In 1984, Barbie got her first high fashion partnership with designer Oscar de la Renta. He was known for creating glamorous runway and red carpet looks. Oscar de la Renta put together shiny, jewel-toned, outfits that sparked creativity and imagination in young fashion lovers.

DID YOU KNOW? Oscar de la Renta was the first of many high fashion partnerships for Barbie.

Andy Warhol

Andy Warhol was a famous American artist best known for his *Campbell's Soup Cans* painting. His pieces often took ordinary objects and turned them into art.

In 1986, Warhol wanted to paint one of his inspirations, BillyBoy*. BillyBoy* was a fashion designer and **socialite**. He was also a big fan of Barbie. He owned 11,000 Barbie dolls! However, BillyBoy* didn't want to be painted. Instead, he told Warhol to paint Barbie. It was Warhol's final piece. He died the next year.

In the 1980s, people went to aerobics classes or exercised at home with workout videos. Athletic wear became its own special **trend**. Mattel took part in the trend when they released Great Shape Barbie and Ken. Barbie was dressed in a full-body turquoise leotard and cozy leg warmers! She looked just like the starlet Jane Fonda who made her own exercise videos.

Great Shape Barbie, 1983

CHAPTER 4

Iconic Barbies

Before 1980, Mattel had released dolls of color as Barbie's friends. The company had never released a doll of color named Barbie. In 1980, the first Black and Hispanic Barbies became available. They each had their own personalities and styles separate from the original Barbie.

COMPLETE AN ACTIVITY HERE!

Hispanic Barbie, 1980

Kitty Black Perkins

Kitty Black Perkins was Mattel's first Black designer. She became the lead designer in 1978. During her long career at Mattel, Perkins hired more people of color to work for the company. Perkins created the first **multicultural** dolls named Barbie. She designed Black Barbie to be different than original Barbie. It helped make Barbie relatable to children of color.

Black Barbie, 1980

Kitty Black Perkins

Mattel had been selling Barbies outside of the US since 1959. In 1981, Mattel began its Dolls of the World collection. Seventeen dolls were released during the decade, including Italian, Mexican, and Korean Barbie. Now girls from all over the world could see themselves reflected in their favorite toy.

Mexican Barbie, 1989

In 1985, Mattel released Day-to-Night Barbie. This doll celebrated women in the workforce. Day-to-Night Barbie was an **executive**. Her day look included a hot pink suit with padded shoulders, stylish hat, briefcase, and calculator. With little effort, Barbie's day look could change into a sparkly and fluffy dress for a night out after work. This Barbie showed young girls they could have it all!

Day-to-Night Barbie, 1985

The glamour of the 1980s was easy to get lost in! MTV brought stars into the home. Female pop stars, such as Madonna and Whitney Houston, were taking over the airwaves! Mattel released Barbie and the Rockers in 1986. This Barbie had big hair, big sleeves, and an even bigger stage presence.

Barbie and the Rockers were a band of five dolls. Alongside Barbie was Dee Dee, Diana, Diva, and Derek.

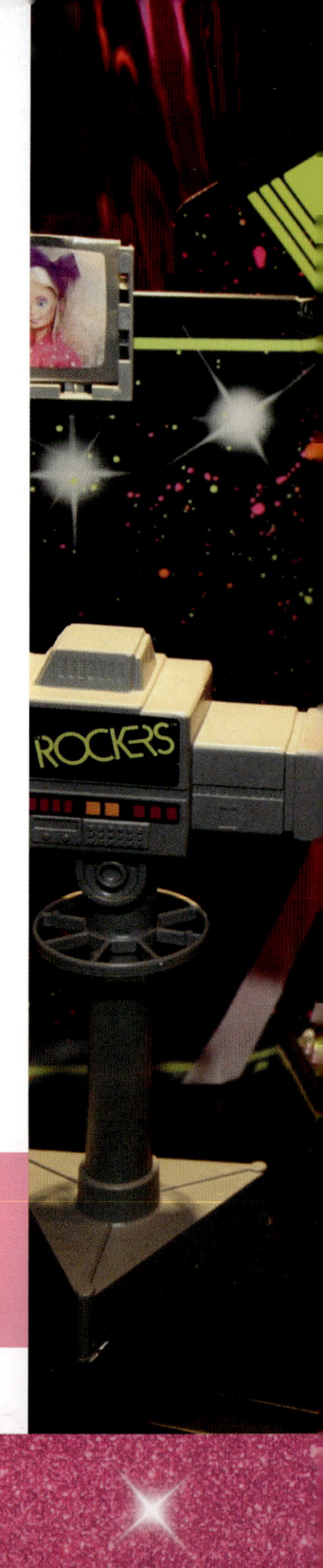

THE ROCKERS

27

28

Astronaut Barbie was released in 1985. She came in a box that said, "We girls can do anything!"

Barbies were bold and bright in the 1980s. Mattel found new and creative ways to inspire children. The next decade would be even bigger and better!

Music Lovin' Tempo Barbie, 1985

Making Connections

TEXT-TO-SELF

Have you ever played with Barbie or her friends? If so, what kind of life did you imagine for them? If not, what kind of life would you imagine?

TEXT-TO-TEXT

Have you read any books about other toys? What did those toys have in common with Barbie? How were they different?

TEXT-TO-WORLD

Sandra Day O'Connor was the first woman to serve on the US Supreme Court. With the help of an adult, research some famous rulings the Supreme Court has made. Write a few sentences explaining a ruling you are interested in.

Glossary

baby boomers — a generation of people born from about 1946 to 1964.

executive — one that directs or controls an organization.

homemaking — caring for a household by cooking, cleaning, and raising children.

hostage — a person captured by another person or group in order to make a deal with authorities.

materialism — an intense focus on material goods.

multicultural — of different cultures. Culture is the customs, arts, and ideas of a group of people.

pager — a small radio receiver that alerts the user to an incoming message.

socialite — a person, usually with a wealthy background, who is famous for their lifestyle.

trend — a current style or preference especially concerning clothing.

Index

Barbie and the Rockers, 26
Barbie Learns to Cook, 9
BillyBoy*, 20
Black Barbie, 22, 23

Crystal Barbie, 18

Day-to-Night Barbie, 25
Dolls of the World, 24
de la Renta, Oscar, 19
dreamhouse, 8

Golden Dream Barbie, 18
Great Shape Barbie, 21

Handler, Ruth, 6, 8–9
Hispanic Barbie, 22

Mattel, 6–8, 21, 22, 23, 24–26, 29
MTV, 13, 16

O'Connor, Sandra Day, 15
original Barbie, 4, 7, 9, 22, 23

Peaches 'n Cream Barbie, 18
Perkins, Kitty Black, 23

Reagan, Ronald, 15

Suburban Shopper Barbie, 9

Warhol, Andy, 20
Women's Rights Movement, 15

DiscoverRoo! ONLINE RESOURCES

This book is filled with videos, puzzles, games, and more! Scan the QR codes* while you read, or visit the website below to make this book pop.

popbooksonline.com/eighties

*Scanning QR codes requires a web-enabled smart device with a QR code reader app and a camera.